Zen Pig

Book 3

All That Is Needed

written by:

mark brown

illustrated by:

amy lynn larwig

Spread the love with...
#ZenPig

Dedicated to you - the reader.

Changing the world by nurturing
the seeds of compassion, gratitude,
and mindfulness.

After a long hot summer,
It was that time of year,
For the festival of thanks
Full of excitement and cheer.

The whole town was gathered
And they asked Zen Pig to speak.
Smiling brightly, he accepted
And began his small speech.

Festival of Thanks

"Each and every one of us,
Could count our blessings all day
Yet never come to an end
Or run out of 'Thank You's' to say.

When we recall all that we have,
All that we have becomes enough.
Happiness cannot be won
Just by getting more stuff.

When it comes to our thanks
Remember this small fact,
There's someone with less
Wishing for what you already have.

Nothing's too small
To recognize and admire
As a gift, a treasure.
Nothing's left to desire.

Discover the joy
Of not wanting more.
Acknowledge your blessings
And your spirit will soar.

Too many before us
Have come, gone, and lost,
Only to discover
The chasing was not worth the cost.

All that you have
Is all that you need
To live the life you want,
Be happy, and succeed.

So sit back and relax,
If only for a moment.
Awaken to your wealth
And let your heart open.

Raise your tea to the sky
And repeat after me,
'I am abundant and happy,
I have all that I need.'"

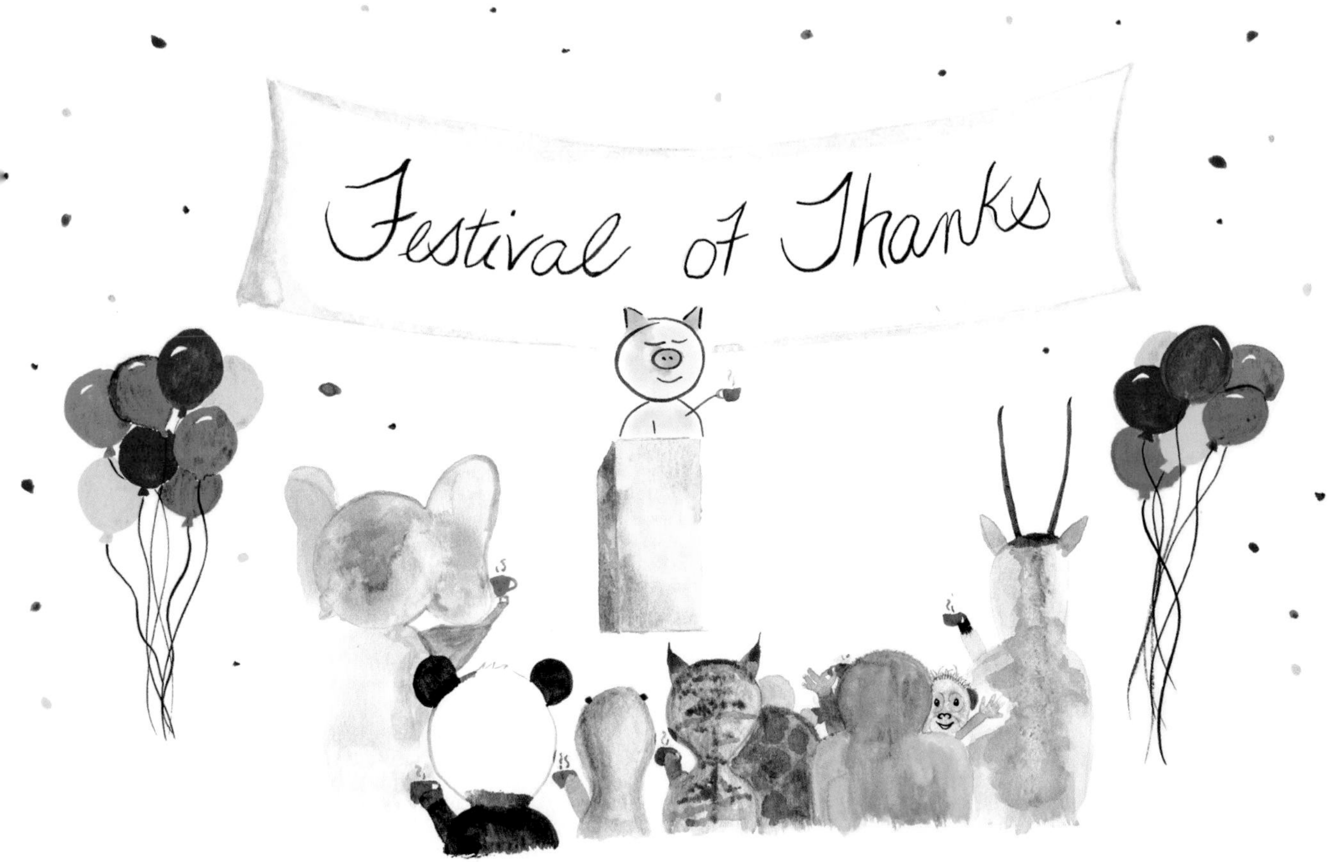
Festival of Thanks

Namaste.

("The light in me loves the light in you.")

Name: _____

Age: _____   Date: _____

Zen Pig's Question:

YOU have many talents.
What talents are you grateful to have?

_____

_____

_____

_____

_____

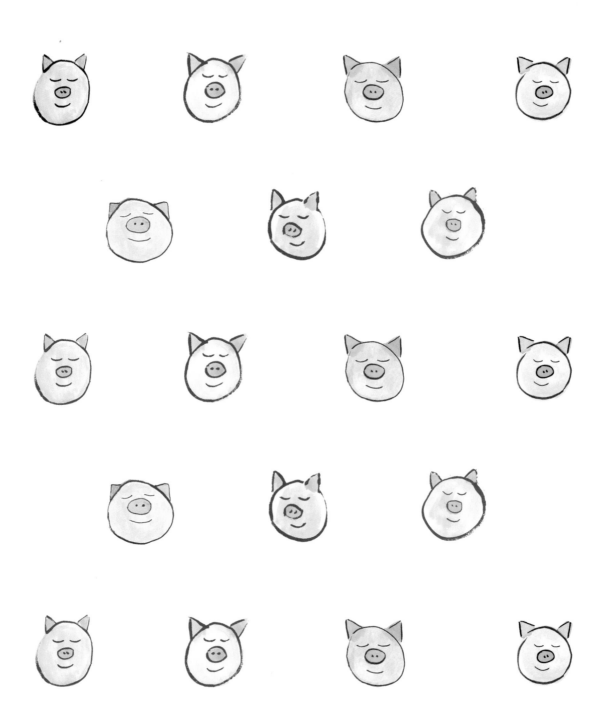